Growing from Potential to Performance:

Creating Transformation by the Renewing of Your Mind

30 Days of Inspiration
30 Learning Lessons
30 Reflection Activities

Doreen M. Lecheler

© 2020 by VisionLinked. Inc.

Doreen M. Lecheler
Growing from Potential to Performance:
Creating Transformation by the Renewing of Your Mind

All rights reserved. No part of this publication may be reproduced, stored in a retrieval system or transmitted in any form or by any means, electronic, mechanical, photocopying, recording or otherwise without the prior permission of the publisher or in accordance with the provisions of the Copyright, Designs and Patents Act 1988 or under the terms of any licence permitting limited copying issued by the Copyright Licensing Agency.

Published by: VisionLinked, Inc.

Text and Cover Design by: Megan Wilbur

Cover Graphics by: Nic Lecheler

Cover Photograph by: Kari HogLund

ISBN-13: 978-1-7336902-0-1

Printed and bound in the United States of America

WELCOME

CREATING & MAINTAINING MEANINGFUL CHANGE

Why do some people experience continual success and fulfillment while others get stuck or struggle along? Science and theology agree that we're born with unlimited potential to grow, change, and develop. Yet what you possess in potential and what you actually achieve in life rarely match up.

High performers and healthy individuals know how to bridge that gap. They don't excel because they have more energy, willpower, or luck. They succeed because they're effective at managing their mind.

Research shows the root of all human behavior begins in the mind with the way you think. Yet few people make a habit of thinking about what they think about. They will invest time, energy, resources, and money to learn more information about personal, professional, and spiritual development, but don't go that extra step of creating transformation – the internal process of becoming the change they long for so they can sustain success and significance at higher levels of living.

CONGRATULATIONS! You've chosen to embark on a 30-day transformation process that will give you knowledge, tools, and insights into how your mind works so you can be more effective at managing the change necessary to live the life you really want.

Using research from neurocognitive science, you'll gain personal awareness into the factors that have been holding you back, as well as techniques for overcoming those hidden roadblocks to abundant life and victorious living. You'll be learning the psychology of success and sustainable results in a fun, enlightening, and deeply motivating way. And the best news is this: you can come back to these lessons again and again to continuously upgrade your level of thinking, behavior, and destiny any time you're ready to grow.

The biggest challenge most people encounter is how they approach this information. Will you simply read this book for knowledge and inspiration, or will you engage with the reflection activities to gain personal insights into your roadblocks to meaningful change and growth in your own life? It ultimately comes down to the difference between gaining new information and creating sustainable transformation. That's why I've outlined this book as a 30-day reflective guide for you.

Socrates said, "The unexamined life is not worth living." The ancient psalmist wrote, "Search me, O God, and know my heart; test me and know my anxious thoughts. See if there is any offensive way in me, and lead me in the way of everlasting" (Psalm 139:23-24, The Holy Bible, NIV). Famed columnist Ann Landers penned, "Know yourself. Don't accept your dog's admiration as conclusive evidence that you're wonderful."

Research shows there's no growth without the first step of self-examination. The reflection activities in this book are designed to get you to dig deep and uncover the root of what's driving your current behaviors yielding your current outcomes. The more time you spend getting to the root of your current thinking, the more targeted and effective your change will become. Once you gain the necessary insights, it becomes a simple process of learning how to retrain your subconscious thinking patterns to take control and manage what's been managing you!

Building a daily habit of guided examination to challenge your current thinking and discovering deeper self-awareness by thoughtfully writing out your responses will make all the difference in how fast you see yourself moving closer toward your goals. This 10-minute-a-day exercise each morning will be your first step to successful change and development in the area(s) of your choosing.

A few recommendations for how to get the most out of this scientific and deeply transformational process:

1. Don't make it your goal to get through the book. Make your goal the outcome you want to see, feel, or possess as a result of going through this process. In the first lesson, you'll be asked to identify a specific goal, activity, or behavior you want to change or reach by the end of 30 days. This will become your focus and intention over the entire process. Having a clear target is essential to success. If you aim at nothing, you can count on hitting nothing every time. Therefore, be specific about the change you want to see. While you're quite capable of changing in multiples areas of your life at the same time, I would encourage you to select one specific goal for the next 30 days. Commit and see it through. Then, as you become more comfortable with the process and familiar with the psychological tools and concepts, you can always go back and address other areas where you'd like to grow.

If you miss a day, that's fine. No pressure. No guilt. Don't put this journey on a "have to" basis. Research shows that living life or business with a "I have to…" mindset only creates more stress and anxiety. When that happens, you'll find yourself procrastinating or pushing back from completing the process.

Give yourself grace and permission. Commit to a "want to" experience as you look forward to the daily self-discovery and internal mindset shift that takes place over a 30-day investment period.

An effective way to create a "want-to" experience is to envision your specific end result as already achieved or accomplished. Then challenge yourself to list all the benefits or "want to's" for accomplishing that change – physically, emotionally, relationally, spiritually, financially, and so on. In other words, why do you want this goal? What do you hope to achieve by gaining it? List as many benefits as possible.

Write your end result and benefits on a 3 x 5 card and keep it close by. Review your card each morning upon rising and before you go to sleep at night. The picture of your end result and the emotions or pay value in achieving it will become so compelling that it will motivate you to invest the 10 minutes each day to move you forward toward your future on a consistent basis.

2. The format of this book is based on research and best practices for successful growth and change. So, discipline yourself to only one lesson per day. Faster isn't necessarily better when it comes to self-examination and change. You actually benefit less by taking on multiple days and lessons at one time rather than letting your spirit and subconscious

fully work one lesson, complete with reflection questions and activities over the course of your day.

Additionally, the process of this book is not only to create self-discovery – the first step to all meaningful and lasting change – it's to create new habit formation. Research indicates that it takes approximately 21-28 days of consistent, focused, reflective thinking to create a new belief in the neuron cell of the brain. Repetitive thought builds belief. The more you dwell on what it is you want - in the proper way – the greater your likelihood of achieving it. The process of revisiting various aspects of your goal over the next 30 days will help you build that daily discipline and new belief.

3. Because you are fluid and ever-changing, and the circumstances around your life are fluid and ever-changing, the lessons and exercises in this book can be applied to your life over and over again – month after month or year after year.

You will not learn all there is about the human mind or gain complete insight into how and why you behave like you do from one reading of this book at this one particular season of your life. However, if you consistently apply these cognitive principles to your daily circumstances – whatever they may be – you will experience an unfolding of insight that will help to propel you forward. You will cultivate the best practices and mindset used by most high-performing individuals that of developing a greater conscious awareness of your subconscious thinking patterns.

To that end, I encourage you to use this book time and again to breathe fresh life into stale outcomes.

4. Lastly, the daily format is constructed by intent. People learn better and retain more effectively when information is presented in story. An intriguing or inspirational narrative opens each day and is designed to impact your thinking and help with recall throughout the day. The developmental principle or cognitive concept will follow and help illustrate the point of the story. Then you'll be asked to reflect on how that lesson applies to your current reality and future goal. I hope you find the flow engaging, interesting, and enlightening. With these recommendations in mind, I wish you all the best as you embark on your **30-Day Journey from Potential to Performance!**

DAY ONE

You and Improved!

STORY - There once was a timid mouse who felt small, afraid, and insignificant. He looked at the courage, accomplishments, and attributes of all the other animals in the jungle, and he desperately wanted more. One day, he learned about a mighty Wizard who had great powers to grant wishes. So he left the comfort of his home in search of the one who could finally make him happy and change his life forever.

Months passed, but the timid mouse finally stood on the steps of the great Wizard's dwelling. With all the courage he could muster, he pleaded, "Oh great and mighty Wizard, if only I could be faster, smarter, and more cunning like my nemesis, the fox. Wizard, can you turn me into a fox?" So the Wizard complied.

One week later, the mouse-turned-fox was back at the Wizard's door. "Oh kind Wizard, if only I could be bigger, stronger, and more regal like my nemesis, the lion. Please, Wizard, can you make me into a lion?" So the Wizard agreed and turned him from a fox to a lion.

Well, only days went by when the lion returned. "Oh great and generous Wizard, if only I could be smarter and more powerful like my nemesis, man. Wizard, I need your powers to make me become a man."

And with that, the Wizard cast forth his powers and turned him back into a mouse, saying, "Though you possess the stature of a lion, you still possess the heart and mind of a mouse."

[Adaptation from a Hindu Folktale]

CONCEPT - As I've consulted with all types of organizations in all parts of the country to increase individual and collective performance, I've found most people try hard to walk and talk like the person they want to be on the outside without doing the necessary work of becoming that person on the inside.

That may work for a while, but stress and anxiety eventually overload your system when you try hard to be better or different than you know yourself to be. If how you think and feel on the inside doesn't match your personae on the outside, change cannot last. And you will never unleash the fullness of your potential.

All successful, sustainable, transformational change must begin on the inside first – in your mind and emotions – so you can naturally and consistently raise your performance to the next level.

But managing who we are isn't so easy. Most of us have never been taught how we think; how the mind works; how beliefs and emotions get in there; how they affect our performance and perception; and how to effectively change them. It's hard to harness something you know little about.

In order to turn your amazing potential into lasting performance, I would like to invite you to select one area of your life to work on over these next 30 days. It could be your health and fitness, finances, a personal characteristic, a relationship or a new skill; perhaps your spiritual life or enhancing your career.

The process and principles you're about to experience, coupled with your growing insights and self-awareness, will give you the tools and techniques over these next 30 days for managing successful growth and sustainable results in your desired area.

INSIGHT - Select an area for desired growth over these next 30 days. Dig deep and be exhaustive in your responses below. The clearer, more descriptive of a picture you give yourself, the better your long-term results will be.

What is your current challenge or issue?

What is it you'd specifically like to change?

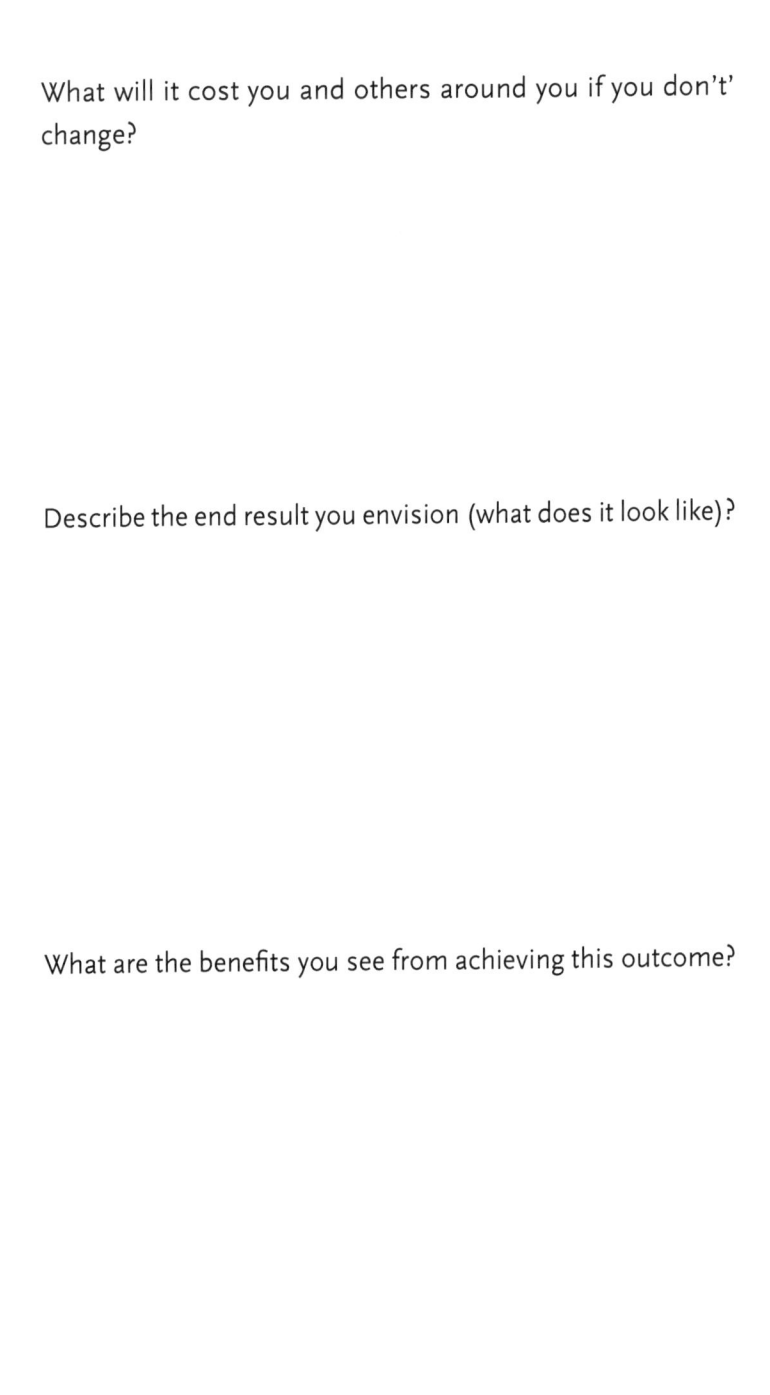

What will it cost you and others around you if you don't' change?

Describe the end result you envision (what does it look like)?

What are the benefits you see from achieving this outcome?

With your specific target area in mind, I'll show you proven steps to grow bigger on the inside so you can perform consistently better on the outside. Tomorrow I'll share the very first thing your mind does every time you try to initiate change.

DAY TWO

UNLEASHING YOUR POTENTIAL

STORY - Did you know your brain contains over 100 billion cells making over 100 trillion computations per second, and no two cells are the same?

You have 100,000 miles of blood vessels, capillaries, and other transport systems in the brain that, when stretched out, can travel around the entire globe four times!

If you were to stretch out just one of your cells, end to end, you would have approximately six feet of DNA code inside that one cell. And if you unraveled that code, there would be approximately 80 billion miles of instruction.

Amazingly, the mechanics that make you uniquely YOU take place in a tiny three pound mass set securely in the nine inches between your ears!

As the ancient wisdom writer declared, you are "fearfully and wonderfully made!"

CONCEPT - Research in the area of human behavior and potential states that you and I have an unlimited capacity to grow, change, and develop. And yet, what we possess in potential paired against what we actually accomplish in life rarely matches up.

That's because each time you encounter new opportunities, information, tasks, challenges, or change, the first thing your subconscious mind tries to evaluate is: "Can I do this? Am I qualified? Do I have what it takes?" How you subconsciously answer those questions has everything to do with the release of your potential.

If your efficacy - your confidence in your ability to handle it or make the change – is high in that particular instance, you'll jump right on it. But if your automatic, instantaneous, subconscious assessment of the situation is low, you'll back away or back down – even if you possess the potential to handle it.

The challenge is this: we don't act and behave at the level of our God-given potential; we act and behave at the level of our beliefs. And in many areas of our life, we are living far below the raw potential we actually possess – physically, mentally, spiritually, relationally, educationally, professionally, and so on.

The sheer physiology of your brain and body, alone, should be conclusive evidence enough that you are, indeed, fearfully and wonderfully made. So let me ask you: Do you believe it? Do you really believe it?

INSIGHT - Spend time today thinking about your end result goal. Thoughtfully and honestly ask yourself:

Do I currently possess the potential to make this change I desire?

If "Yes," why haven't I already accomplished or possess my desired end result?

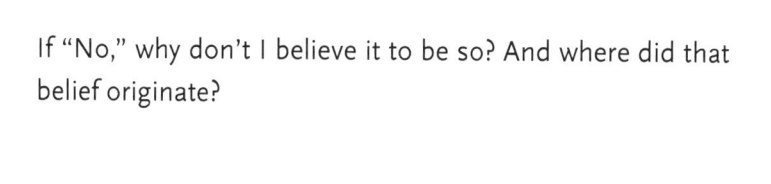

If "No," why don't I believe it to be so? And where did that belief originate?

"Whether you think you can or you think you can't, you're probably right." Henry Ford's famous quote couldn't be more true! How you manage your mind directly impacts your outcomes. But it's hard to manage something you know little about. So tomorrow we'll begin to explore the nature of potential.

DAY THREE

What Lies Below the Surface

STORY - April 10, 1912 marked an epic event. It was the maiden voyage of the world's largest, most renowned, luxury-class ocean liner afloat – the RMS Titanic.

It left Southampton, UK bound for New York City carrying 2, 224 passengers and crew. Four days into the crossing, the Titanic struck an iceberg, buckling the ship's hull plates and filling it with water. In less than two hours, the ship sank killing more than two-thirds of the people aboard. Only 705 souls survived.

Estimates on the iceberg's size ranged from 50 to 100 feet high and 200 to 400 feet long, but those figures related to the size seen above the water. Picture this: 85-90% of an iceberg's total potential lies below the surface. Using those percentages, the iceberg's mass was between 1 and 3 million square feet of hidden, perilous ice.

A big reason the sailors missed the iceberg is exactly that – they failed to realize they were only looking at 10% of the potential that lay ahead of them. Had they understood the full enormity of the iceberg, they certainly would have made haste to avoid it.

CONCEPT - In much the same way, we often under-estimate the size of our own potential by fixating on the circumstances and outcomes we see around us rather than what we possess within us. We focus on what is seen and call it "truth" or "reality" rather than on what is unseen – the potential that lies below.

The sum of your potential is not merely what's measurable on the surface - your conscious-level behaviors and achievements. They represent about 5% of what's possible. In fact, science tells us 95-99% of your daily activities are driven by subconscious impulses and programmed beliefs.

So instead of trying to squeeze more out of your conscious-level 5%, you'll realize far greater strides by harnessing the untapped power in the hidden, subconscious factors that actually drive your behavior.

Yes, natural-born abilities, learned skills, and education all effect performance. But your real leverage lies in learning how to identify and navigate the roadblocks you've unknowingly erected below the surface.

INSIGHT - If failure was not an option, what would you look like, feel like, and act like once you accomplished your maiden journey (your defined goal). Be specific and choose vivid words that excite you.

What would I look like to others?

What would I act like?

What would I feel like when it's accomplished?

Reflect on these "look like," "act like," "feel like" images throughout the day, and begin to see your attitudes and actions begin to change.

You can't effectively change the direction of your outcomes without knowing what's driving them below the surface. And though the mass of your potential is often bigger than you think, your worldview impacts your ability to release it. Tomorrow we'll look at one important factor that shifts your potential into high performance.

DAY FOUR

Who's In Control?

STORY - I was working with the executive team of a major transportation company in the U.S. to create a culture of excellence. The leadership was very open and eager to implement these high performance tools. They worked hard, and soon saw a huge return on investment.

A year later, one Senior Vice President left to head up a smaller transportation company. He was a warm, charismatic, constructive President and CEO. Using all he had learned from our engagement, he now worked tirelessly to encourage high performance among his people. But no matter how hard he tried, they wouldn't assume leadership responsibilities on their own. Astounded and exhausted, he finally asked for help.

When I assessed their culture, I found the former CEO was highly autocratic. He barked the orders. You did what you were told to do, and beware if you blew it. He had conditioned his people with fear-based motivation and restrictive behaviors.

Now that the autocratic CEO was gone, and a more constructive leader was in place, the opportunity was theirs for the taking. The problem was they couldn't own it. They just couldn't see themselves assuming accountability for their own decisions and the organization's success. They now had all the potential, but didn't know how to use it.

CONCEPT - It's hard to empower people who have relinquished possession of their future.

When this happens, it's often so subtle that we're not even aware. We may look accomplished on the outside but have internal scars reminding us we have no control.

Some people experience external circumstances – good or bad – and know they're accountable and responsible for their own internal responses, happiness, and success. They have what all high performing individuals possess – an internal locus of control.

Conversely, those with an external locus of control keep waiting for the world to change on the outside so they'll feel better about themselves on the inside. They place the accountability and responsibility for their health, happiness, safety, security, promotion, and so on, on the people and things around them.

Understanding that choice of response always belongs to you is essential for successful change. Life happens, and you can't always control the things around you. But you can control what you will do with them. Nothing can crush you without your consent.

INSIGHT - Ask yourself: Is it inside me or outside me that will make the difference?

Is there something from my past conditioning that has caused me to relinquish control of my future in particular areas of my life?

Where am I currently waiting for others to support or propel me forward?

What beliefs must I change to strengthen my internal locus of control?

We've all had experiences growing up that influenced the worldview we hold today. In turn, our worldview influences how we perceive, interpret, and respond to the current circumstances around us.

In areas where we're under-living our potential, it's important to consider whether we're giving up accountability to external factors outside us. One way to determine that is to listen to when or where you blame others for your lack of happiness, success, health, peace, purpose, and more.

In order to unleash more potential, you must possess a strong, internal locus of control that believes — no matter the circumstances - "If it's to be, it's up to me." [William H. Johnsen]

With that directive and determination, we'll look, tomorrow, at the first step necessary for all successful and sustainable change to take place.

DAY FIVE

Live Consciously

STORY - I read a book by best-selling author Laurie Beth Jones in which she shared a story that struck quite close to my own experience with "incurable" metastatic cancer.

In the book she told the story about a woman who was diagnosed with late stage, terminal cancer. Her husband noticed how she began living with deeper clarity and love.

As she neared the end, he finally worked up the courage to ask her, "What does it feel like living each day knowing you're dying?"

She turned to him and replied, "What does it feel like living each day pretending you're not."

CONCEPT - We all have them - liberating beliefs that open opportunities and limiting beliefs that block us from being, seeing, and having more. How you think matters.

Socrates said, "The unexamined life is not worth living." Why? Research tells us it's your thoughts, habits, attitudes, and expectations, at the root cause level, that drive your behaviors.

It takes conscious intention and constant attention if you want to live with greater success, significance, clarity, and love. It begins with becoming consciously aware of the subconscious thinking patterns dominating and directing your life.

There is no growth without the first step of mindful, self-reflection in relation to the goal or outcome you hope to achieve.

INSIGHT - Today - open your awareness to the thoughts, words, and feelings that cross your mind. Make a note of where and when you entertain:

Lack versus Abundance

"Can't" versus "Can"

"No" versus Yes"

"Impossible versus "All things are possible"

Where and when do you sense your emotions surging throughout the day? What people, activities or circumstances seem to set them off?

How do you rebound or regroup in those situations?

If you're thinking directly impacts your performance, then shouldn't you be spending more time thinking about what you think about? Once you identify and understand what's holding you back, then it's a simple process of managing your mind for the life you long to live.

But first, that requires an understanding of how the mind works. Tomorrow we'll look at one of the functions of your mind that keeps you acting like you.

DAY SIX

Taking Out the Trash

STORY - A 1960's phrase originating from computer science and communications technology became widely adapted into leadership, management, and decision-making circles. "Garbage In/Garbage Out" referred to the erroneous data entered into a computer. If the input is inaccurate, you can count on the output being incorrect.

Applying this principle to human psychology, your mind is like a computer. It accepts and records the information you give it and stores it at the subconscious level, never to be lost.

The mind is also amoral - it doesn't debate the data. If you tell yourself, "I'll never get ahead; I can't lose weight; I don't remember names;" your mind simply imprints that information, along with the emotion, into the neuron cells of your brain.

In turn, these beliefs accumulate to form your self-image – what you know to be "true" about you, regardless of the real potential you might actually possess. We don't naturally, consistently behave at the level of our potential. We act and behave according to the image we believe to be true about ourselves.

Like a computer, your output – performance – will match the input of data you've given it. If you want new and better outputs, then it's essential you give yourself new and better inputs that are more aligned with what you hope to achieve.

CONCEPT - Regardless of the depth of your desires or the raw potential you possess, it's the quality of your thoughts that dictate the quality of your life. Inflicted and infected thinking is the poison at the root of your potential.

Interestingly, most of the data you have stored about yourself wasn't put there by intent. It was the opinions and attitudes of others that you accepted and recorded along your life journey, even if it was hurtful and harmful to you.

Like the smell of garbage, there's a name for these negative, limiting thoughts; it's called "stinkin-thinkin."

INSIGHT - In what areas of your life are you not experiencing the sweet smell of success and satisfaction?

Consider what "garbage" you may have accepted about yourself that's souring your dreams and desires.

Identify beliefs you no longer wish to keep. Write them down and commit to throwing them out.

The objective of self-examination is to data-mine inaccurate, ineffective thinking that's no longer serving you. Simply ignoring or pushing through it won't work. Like a computer virus, you must address it before it infects your entire system.

Tomorrow we'll dig deeper into the types of misinformation you've assimilated so you can unlock the reservoir of unlimited potential within.

DAY SEVEN

What's Your Truth?

STORY - In 1983, at age 61, Australian potato farmer, Albert Ernest Clifford Young, made history. He entered a 544-mile ultra-marathon competition between Sydney and Melbourne, running against the best in the world. He drew obvious media attention when he arrived new to the sport in overalls and wading boots and ran with an unusual gait.

He trailed behind seasoned runners for most of the first day, but eventually Cliff Young completed the race. In fact, he did more than that – he actually won the race against these younger, world-class athletes. Ultimately, he finished in a staggering five days, fifteen hours and four minutes - almost two days faster than the previous world record! How did he do it?

When interviewed, they found Cliff won the race, not because he was faster, but because he didn't sleep. You see, the prevailing truth or belief among runners was that sleep was absolutely essential for a race that long. But Young, being a farmer and not a marathoner, didn't travel in circles where he heard that truth. So while the others were sleeping, Cliff Young kept running.

Think about that.... He was able to beat the record by almost two full days, not because he was faster or better at running, but simply because he didn't subscribe to the same information everyone else did.

CONCEPT - The outcomes you're now experiencing are the result of your best thinking at this moment. If you change the way you think, you'll change the way you run your life.

The challenge is this: All information, experiences, and emotions you've ever encountered are stored in your subconscious mind. You call them "truth" or "reality." And you're hard-wired to behave according to those truths as you believe them to be. That's called sanity.

In the makings of the mind, maintaining sanity is more important than experiencing success. So who's giving you your "truths," and are those beliefs helping you win the marathon of life?

INSIGHT - Reflect on this question today:

"If I have the desire and I have the potential, why have I not yet accomplished my focus area goal?"

Write down all responses that surface. Then examine each and ask, "Is this really true? Why do I believe so? Where did this (these) belief(s) originate?"

Your mind records the information you give it as truth or reality. Even when you desire to grow, one function of your creative subconscious is to keep you acting like you. It's called sanity.

Change requires more than willpower; it begins with a re-evaluation of the things you know as 'truth" about yourself, your industry, others, and the world.

Tomorrow we'll identify a second factor that's impacting your current level of performance.

DAY EIGHT

"What I Feared Most Has Come Upon Me"

STORY - Rutgers University did one of the first longevity studies on perspective and wellness. They took older adults – same ages; same health profiles – but split them into two groups.

Group one complained of everyday aches, pains, and problems. They were generally more pessimistic about their health and their future. Conversely, group two saw themselves as healthy, active, and vibrant toward life.

After following each group over a ten-year period, the evidence was clear. Though participants began with similar health profiles, those with the negative expectations became more sedentary, less social, more sick, more medicated, and had more hospital visits than the optimistic group.

Even more poignant in their findings was this: those who expected to live a long and healthy life, were healthier, happier, and actually outlived the negative group by 5-7 years.

CONCEPT - You can't dwell in one perspective and expect the benefits of another. Why? You move toward what you think about.

What you behold, you become. What you magnify, you eventually manifest – even down to your physiology.

Research shows we don't get what we want; we get what we expect. We draw people and opportunities to ourselves we feel worthy of receiving.

If you expect a bad day, you'll see it or subconsciously cause it for yourself. Better known as the self-fulfilling prophecy, your mind is actually looking for information to match your expectations and prove that you're not crazy for believing what you believe to be true. More than that, it filters out information that contradicts what you expect to see. So, what are you looking for today?

INSIGHT - In relation to your goal, write down what people, opportunities, skills, and resources you'll need to accomplish and sustain your envisioned outcome. Examine what expectations you currently hold about each? Be honest.

Which expectations will lead to your goal? Which ones need to change?

When I coach or speak with individuals diagnosed with cancer, I find most people hope and pray one thing – healing- but dwell on and talk about the other – the disease. It's a prescription for disaster!

The psychology of human behavior and performance tells us that we act and move in the direction of our most dominant ideas.

If you expect misfortune, you will find it. If you want success, set your expectations on success.

DAY NINE

THE COST OF ATTITUDES

STORY - As Vice President of Development for an international humanitarian organization, I had many responsibilities, including fundraising.

I excelled at grant writing, special events, marketing materials, media relations, and donation appeal letters. But I noticed how uncomfortable I was meeting directly with our donor base. I would procrastinate over simply contacting them. Though passionate about communicating our work, I'd avoid the direct "ask" for their financial support. I was hoping my enthusiasm would simply move them to give greater amounts.

It bothered me that my colleagues in other nonprofit fields loved asking for money. They felt it was a privilege. They believed people who loved your mission wanted and expected to be asked to give and give big as a way of partnering with you to help advance the mission.

So why didn't I feel that way? I knew the same tools of the trade as my fundraising colleagues knew. I had as much potential as they did to be successful.

Rather than accept my uncomfortable feelings as "truth," I decided to dig deeper to understand the root cause "why." I remembered how my father was obsessively frugal. We were taught it wasn't polite to discuss money. When my parents divorced, constant arguments surfaced over the subject.

Subconsciously, I adopted deep-seeded attitudes that it was improper, uncomfortable, and even controversial to talk about money.

CONCEPT - It's often our attitudes, not our aptitudes, that determine the heights of our success.

Not only was I robbing myself of my potential as an effective fundraiser, but I was robbing the organization's mission and reach; as well as the donors' sense of partnership in making a difference; and, most importantly, the number of lives we could save in the world. What a costly miscalculation over an uncomfortable attitude with money!

A Hebrew proverb says, "As a man thinks in his heart, so is he."

The attitudes of your heart either draw you in the direction of your desires or distance you from your goals. You cannot achieve success if your attitudes don't align with the outcomes you desire.

INSIGHT - What attitudes do you possess that work against the outcomes you envision?

What people, situations or responsibilities you tend to avoid or dismiss?

Then write down one or two positive, constructive attitudes you'll need in order to accomplish and sustain your goal.

Along with beliefs and expectations, your attitudes are a powerful force controlling the release of your potential. You're not born with attitudes; they're learned responses triggered by emotions that have become automatically programmed in your mindset. They're formed by your interpretation of your own experiences, along with those attitudes you've adopted from others.

Most of the time, we don't question our attitudes. We simply accept them as truth, or tell ourselves, "that's just the way I am," even if they cost us success, well-being, and happiness.

DAY TEN

How to Get Unstuck

STORY - After my first bout with cancer, I decided to run a half-marathon. Surgery and radiation weakened me. Hormone therapy put thirty pounds on my thin frame. More than anything, I was sick of having my body controlled by external sources. I was out to reclaim myself.

At first, I could barely get down to the end of the block and back. But I began training slowly as I worked up my strength and increased my distance. It felt great, and I was seeing results – not only in my athletic performance, but in my physical shape. I felt like I was beginning to see the old me again.

But three-quarters into the training, my body seemed to stall. I completed the half-marathon just fine, but I wasn't continuing to tone and thin down like I expected.

I hired a personal trainer who gave me new exercise routines every week. It felt a bit frustrating, at first. Just as I would get the hang of a new routine, he'd change it up again.

I learned about something called "muscle memory." Through the repetition of movement, the brain/body connection causes muscle to become familiar with the activity.

The good news is this: eventually the habit of movement becomes an unconscious process you don't even have to think about. The bad news is: eventually the habit of movement plateaus further muscle strength and development. You get stuck doing the same thing and getting the same results.

CONCEPT - Habits help create a comfortable routine. But even healthy habits run the risk of killing innovation and continuous improvement.

You know the saying, "If you always do what you've always done, you'll always get what you always got."

The challenge is this: we often tell ourselves it's what we've been doing that's worked so well and created our success. And, likely, it has! But the more routine you are at being good, the harder it is to break into that next level of being great.

Make habits work for you. Establish ones that produce growth. When performance plateaus, recognize the habits you've developed; open your creativity to new ways of doing things; and establish a new set of behaviors. Repeat this each time you feel stuck, and you'll see you've created a new habit called "continuous improvement!"

INSIGHT - Where have you plateaued in your performance? Stuck at the same weight, same job, same finances, same Friday night routine? Are there particular habits you've subconsciously fallen into in relation to your goal area?

If you were to create new "muscle memory," where would you want it to be, and what would you like it to look like?

A human behavior principle states: when you lock on to one particular way of doing or looking at things, you also lock out other potential ways. Locking on is good - it enables action and progress. But unless you eventually open up, the law of diminishing returns sets in.

Habits can enrich or enslave you. They create routinized responses that keep you acting like YOU. So be sure it's the YOU you want to be.

DAY ELEVEN

Making Change Last

STORY - Harvard Business School's Dr. John Kotter is the change management guru and author of "Leading Change." He noted that 70% of business change initiatives fail – either they fail to meet the goal, or fail to sustain it once they arrive. When you consider the amount of time, effort, and resources companies put into making change, a 70% failure rate is a daunting amount of waste and inefficiency.

The same holds true for individual change. For instance, the U.S. weight loss industry touts $30 billion in annual revenue with over 100 million dieters per year. Yet, the National Institute of Health estimates that most dieters regain 66% of their weight loss within a year after completing their diet plan. And within five years, they will have regained all their weight plus additional pounds.

Change is hard. It's often uncomfortable to make and unwelcomed when it arrives, even when the change promises to be better for you.

CONCEPT - Earlier in the process, I mentioned one reason why change feels difficult: It's called "sanity."

One function of your creative subconscious mind is to keep you acting like YOU. That's good news. You don't have to wake each morning and reestablish what kind of person you are – your likes and dislikes, or how you walk and talk. Your creative subconscious does the work of helping you stay like the person you believe yourself to be.

But when you set a goal or encounter situations on the outside that look different from what you know to be true about yourself on the inside (your subconscious reality), the mind goes into self-regulation mode to get you back to what's normal for you.

A second reason change is hard is that most of us go about initiating change the wrong way. We use external means to motivate us without changing the internal idea of who we are.

INSIGHT - Think about the last time you attempted to change in your goal area. If this is your first time, then think back to another instance when you set a goal for change.

Write down all the things you tried – behaviorally and mentally – to get the results you wanted.

How successful were you in reaching the result? Were you able to sustain your desired outcome?

If YES, why do you think so? What was your motivation?

If NO, why not?

When you understand patterns in your successful and unsuccessful change initiatives, it'll be far easier to understand how to move forward with your next change initiative.

Tomorrow I'll show you the most common way we get stuck when trying to create new outcomes in our lives.

DAY TWELVE

Just Do It, Or Else...

STORY - In 1988, a Portland, Oregon ad agency created what would be selected as one of the top two advertising taglines of the entire 20th century. "Just Do It" became a world renowned slogan and trademark for Nike. The success of this campaign increased market shares of Nike's North American business from 18% to 43%, and its worldwide sales skyrocketed from 800 million to 9.2 billion dollars.

Though they used extreme sports and high-level athletes in their advertising, their success was in positioning Nike as fashion wear over fitness wear. Growing the fitness market was significantly more difficult. Why?

If fitness isn't already your dominant mindset, changing shoe wear won't make it so. You can push yourself to do it a time or two, but, eventually, you'll go back to the person you know yourself to be. Fashion, on the other hand, requires far less effort to change.

CONCEPT - Most people use "muscle management" as their motivation for change. Using all their conscious-level willpower and tenacity, they push themselves, push others, and push the circumstances in order to succeed.

Can you get movement from pushing? Sure! But what happens when you get tired, sick, busy, travel, or company comes, and you stop pushing? You stop moving!

Pushing ourselves and others is an external, coercive means of motivation. Through fear, guilt, and intimidation, we try to force behavioral change. It often sounds like this: "I have to do this." "You'd better shape up." "We need to work harder".... all ways of driving behavior through conscious-level willpower.

The problem is this: we all have a subconscious, innate response when being pushed – we instinctively push back – whether you're pushing others to change or you're pushing yourself.

In the areas of your life where you are stalling, stuck, procrastinating, or producing half-hearted results, you may be living your life on a "have to" basis. Get yourself to "want to," and you'll see how motivation and performance soar!

INSIGHT- Where have you tried hard to push yourself or others into behavioral change using coercive means or brut willpower?

Pay attention today to tasks and responsibilities. Make a list of where you tend to respond with I "have to," "should," or "need to."

Take your list and flip the negative, coercive attitudes into positive benefits for getting the task done. List them all. The more you focus on the benefits, the greater your internal motivation responds.

When you externally push yourself into change, essentially, you're trying hard on the outside to be bigger, better, different than you know yourself to be on the inside. With this mindset, change won't last. Once you give up conscious control, you always go back to the subconscious truths you hold about yourself.

Tomorrow we'll look at a second way people lure themselves into change. It's a costly endeavor that's not easily sustained.

DAY THIRTEEN

Eye on the Prize

STORY - When it came to marriage and family, I was a late bloomer. I was 40 years young when my son was born. But as a life-long student and teacher of potential and human behavior, I was going to be the best, most constructive, affirming, encouraging mom I could be. I was, after all, a professional at this.

Well it didn't take long before I was soon doing what most parents (and managers) do to elicit positive behavior. I enticed (or, more nearly, bribed) good behavior out of my son using incentives.

The idea behind incentives is to pull (rather than push) performance from people and have them associate the effort with profitable benefits.

What I soon learned (and hear from most managers I work with) is that incentives don't last. Oh sure, you can get the behavior you want while dangling the carrot in front of their face, but once the prize is gained, the performance is not sustained.

CONCEPT - People like to be recognized and rewarded for good behavior. It's an intrinsic human trait. But incentives, as a means of creating better performance, don't last. The minute the prize or contest is over, you always go back to the person you know yourself to be on the subconscious level.

Moreover, when we use incentives as external motivation, we have to keep upping the ante in order to keep stimulating the desired behavior.

What used to be a piece of candy to motivate my son soon grew into small toys, and then costly video games! The same goes for individuals and organizations.

It's important to celebrate success as a way to build confidence for the future. But if you want long-term performance, you need to adopt a process to develop internal drive and motivation.

INSIGHT - Where have you used incentives to motivate behavior in yourself or others?

How effective was it in maintaining performance at an all-time high?

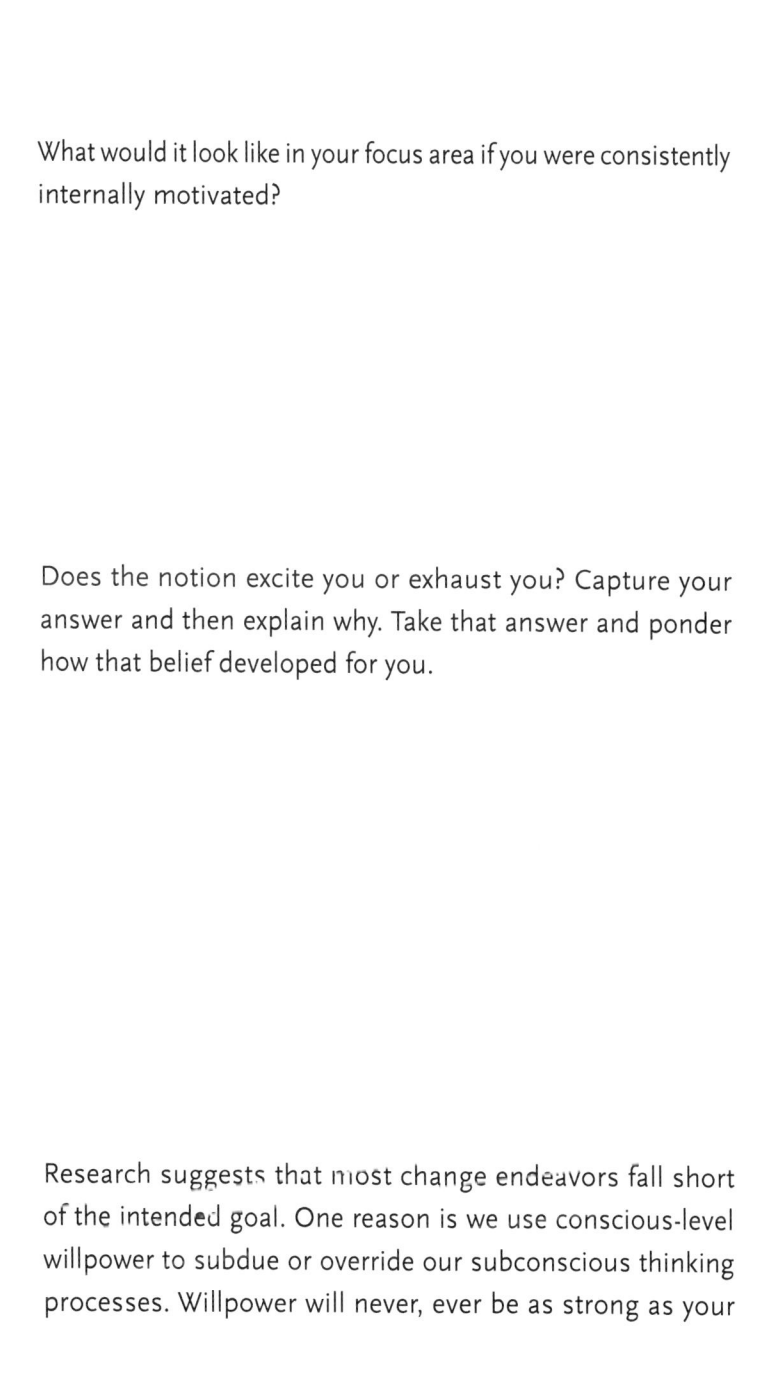

What would it look like in your focus area if you were consistently internally motivated?

Does the notion excite you or exhaust you? Capture your answer and then explain why. Take that answer and ponder how that belief developed for you.

Research suggests that most change endeavors fall short of the intended goal. One reason is we use conscious-level willpower to subdue or override our subconscious thinking processes. Willpower will never, ever be as strong as your subconscious mind. A change of behavior requires a change of perspective...something we'll talk more about tomorrow.

DAY FOURTEEN

Seeing All There is To See

STORY - A wealthy man wanted to teach a lesson to his son, so they went to the farm of a very poor family. When they returned from the day, the father asked, "Did you see how poor people live?"

"Oh yes," said the son.

"So what did you learn?" asked the father.

"Well, I saw that we have one dog, and they had four. We have a pool that reaches to the middle of our garden, and they have a creek that has no end. We have imported lanterns in our garden, and they have the stars at night. Our patio reaches to the front yard, and they have the whole horizon. We have a small piece of land to live on, and they have fields that go beyond our sight. We have servants who serve us, but they serve one another. We buy our food, but they grow theirs. We have walls around our property to protect us; they have friends to protect them."

The boy's father was speechless.

Then his son added, "Thanks, Dad, for showing me how poor we really are."

CONCEPT - We often say "seeing is believing." In fact the opposite is true. Your perspective, or beliefs, actually influence what you see, hear, taste, touch, and smell – the information that gets filtered through your senses and reaches your brain.

An area of your brain called the Reticular Activating System (RAS) has the job of screening information that matches your beliefs. It lets in evidence that confirms your perspective and blocks out all other data as superfluous or unnecessary. It actually builds blind spots to information that's present.

There's simply too much information hitting your senses at any one time – so much so that if you were to filter it all in, you couldn't concentrate. So your RAS works to select two types of information to get through: threat or danger, and data that reinforces what you hold to be true or significant about yourself, others, and the world around you.

Be careful what you tell yourself. You'll see it every time and wonder why you're always so right.

INSIGHT - What opinions do you hold about the people, processes, and possibilities in your focus area?

Now that you know about the Reticular Activating System, consider what perspectives might cause you to become more convinced about the possibilities or impossibilities for your success.

Perspective matters. It's more than just your outlook on life; it actually impacts your intake of information. Your perspective reinforces your reality which, in turn, influences the quality and quantity of information you receive.

If you want to grow your potential into lasting high performance, make it a practice of asking yourself, "Is my perspective supporting or hindering me from achieving my desired goals and the quality of life I desire to live?"

DAY FIFTEEN

What Will You Decide?

STORY - In 2009 I had a recurrence of cancer. It was only 2-1/2 years from the first diagnosis, only now I was told it was stage four, "incurable," with metastases to the bone. One prominent institution told me I'd have about eighteen months until the cancer would spread to the other organs of my body.

Fortunately, I'm a person of deep faith and knew what to think in the midst of disease. And as a professional in neurocognitive behavior, I also had the training and tools for how to think in times of crisis.

What concerned me most was the number of people who receive this kind of devastating news and don't know how to manage their mind. With all the medical professionals I saw, not once...with ANY of them...did they ever ask me what I could do to give healing a chance to take root in my body.

For them, my future wasn't based on the potential of what I could bring to the table; it was based on my diagnosis plus the history of similar others who had gone before me.

CONCEPT - History is an important benchmark in many ways. But we need to be carefully and consciously aware of when it's protecting us from harm or robbing us of hope.

Each time you're confronted with new information, challenges, or opportunities, your mind goes into an instantaneous, automatic, four-step decision-making process that takes place within:

- Step 1 is perception – a conscious awareness of information you see, hear, smell, touch, or taste around you;
- Step 2 is association – the subconscious mind is looking for context and asking if the new information matches anything you've ever seen or experienced before;
- Step 3 is evaluation – based on past associations, what is this new experience likely leading me toward; and
- Step 4 is your conscious-level decision

What we know is most people make decisions, not based on the potential of what can be, but on the history of what has been. That's important – particularly when it comes to touching a hot stove or crossing a busy street. But it can also keep you from taking higher ground and believing "all things are possible to those who believe" ~Jesus Christ.

INSIGHT - What major life events have impacted you?

What emotional or "logical" conclusions have you drawn from them?

How are they helping you move forward? How are they potentially holding you back?

Rather than automatically reacting to the past, envision new ways you can evaluate information in order to better influence future situations. Regardless of how similar the situation is to the past, decide that what's inside you now will help you create a new and better outcome.

We value experience. We believe it gives us knowledge, familiarity, and insight. We hope it make us better, faster, and smarter for the days ahead.

Now that you know your evaluation of new information is based on the outcomes from past associations, you can be more mindful about your decisions to insure they are a potential help and not a hindrance to your future.

DAY SIXTEEN

A Time For Letting Go

STORY - One of the most beautiful musical scores and cinematic movies of all times is The Mission. The film debuted in 1986 starring Robert De Niro, Jeremy Irons, and Liam Neeson. It's an emotionally stirring and visually stimulating drama about a Jesuit mission in South America in the 1700's.

De Niro plays Mendoza, a former slave trader who is now penitent about his life. He returns with the priests to the Mission - the native community high above the falls. As the Jesuits make the perilous climb up the cliffs, Mendoza follows. He drags a heavy, cumbersome bundle of his old armor and weapons, making his ascent up the falls arduous and all the more treacherous.

He struggles and nearly plummets to his death, but he refuses help and refuses to let go. He feels he must carry the weight of his past into his future to remind him of who he used to be.

Mendoza's redemption arrives at the top of falls. The natives who he once persecuted surround him. They pull their knives as they recognize the man who ravaged their village and kidnapped their families. Just as you think they're about to exact their revenge, they cut the rope to release his burden as it plunges into the waters below. It's a profound moment of mercy and forgiveness, and Mendoza is utterly undone by their grace.

CONCEPT - In areas of your life where you feel stuck, you may need to cut the ropes of your past in order to reach the heights of your potential.

You can't ignore or neglect it. The emotional and memory imprint is already stored in the neurons of your brain, never to be erased. More than that, it impacts how you look at and respond to your future. It takes an intentional act of release and a process of replacement to reconcile old hurts into new life.

INSIGHT - Create a quiet space and give yourself some thoughtful time today to think about emotions of fear, worry, anger, sadness, resentment, frustration, disappointment, humiliation or more that you've experienced toward people throughout your life. Begin with your early childhood memories and progress through your life, making a list of each individual and situation where you were pained – even if it seems silly or insignificant today.

Decide today to cut the rope of burden, and move forward in freedom. Name each individual, acknowledge the offense; declare your forgiveness toward the person and release the negative emotion. Be sure to see yourself filling that emotional void with the positive emotion you choose to imprint.

Hanging on to the past is a waste of your future. Letting go is more than a one-time declaration to not let things bother you anymore. In order to seize the opportunities of tomorrow you must be unencumbered by emotional memories of the past.

Some people like to use their negative emotions to fuel their progress. Tomorrow we'll see why, in fact, that's more dangerous than you think.

DAY SEVENTEEN

THE POWER OF EMOTIONS

STORY - Dr. Caroline Leaf, developer of the Metacognitive-Mapping Approach, looks at the physiology of thinking – how thought moves through the brain and body by electrochemical impulses.

Like a relay system, information moves from one section of your brain to another, including your amygdala, the emotion center of your brain. It's looking for old emotional memory that resembles your new circumstances. It stimulates that old emotion and sends it to your hypothalamus – the pumping gland of your endocrine system – which produces chemicals in response to your thought life. Those chemicals then impact your physical response.

Leaf classifies two emotion groups: negative fear-based emotions and positive faith-based emotions – each with their own set of chemical molecules that attach to your cells.

When you feel love, happiness, peace, or satisfaction, serotonin and other feel-good endorphins flush through your body helping to boost your immune system, enhance memory, and build intelligence. On the other hand, anxiety, fear, stress, and anger produce cortisol and adrenaline that are fine for short-term flight or fight situations. But these emotions sustained as a chronic lifestyle block learning, weaken cells, and eventually cause disease.

CONCEPT - Research shows approximately 87% of illnesses have their root causes in how you think. If you don't effectively manage your will and emotions, you'll soon discover they're managing you.

Some people like to use negative experiences to fuel their commitment to succeed. Be careful. While it's helpful to turn bad situations into positive outcomes, emotions like resentment, revenge, and hate actually take up more physical space in the brain, impairing judgment and rational thinking.

Those who claim to work best under pressure actually put their body in chronic stress mode.

And those who think it's better to suppress emotions rather than deal with hurtful experiences disrupt the body's flow of fending off foreign and deadly invaders.

INSIGHT - Which do you resemble more – the quiet worrier or the demonstrative warrior? Though one's considered passive and the other aggressive, they're simply opposite sides of the same coin – FEAR. Peel back the layers of every negative emotion, and you'll find FEAR is the root cause. What are your fears? Make a list.

Think deeply about where each originated. What beliefs or "truths" have you formed as a result?

Dealing with sour emotions isn't just about trying hard to control your attitude. Your emotions are responsible for the very life and health of your body, even down to the cellular level.

You can't live in the fullness of your potential – physically, spiritually, or cognitively – if you don't unearth the fear driving your emotions and behaviors.

Tomorrow, we'll look at how to bring your best thinking and feelings to life.

DAY EIGHTEEN

What Are You Hungry For?

STORY - A young student sat at the feet of an old sage. "Master," he inquired, "I do not understand what I do. For what I want to do I do not do, but what I hate I do."

The old sage smiled, "You're experiencing the battle of the beast within. Outside the sacred place of your heart is a beast out to destroy all that was destined to live there."

"What was destined to live there," asked the student?

"Love, joy, peace, patience, kindness, goodness, gentleness, faithfulness, and self-control.

The beast lives on hate, fear, anxiety, envy, anger, bitterness, selfishness, lust, and revenge."

"Oh Sage, how can I kill this beast within?"

The old sage quietly replied, "Stop feeding him."

CONCEPT - Most often, it's our mental enemies that become our mortal enemies. It's essential to know that regardless of what people tell you or the circumstances that arise, choice of response is yours and yours alone.

I often say of cancer that it's more a battle of the mind than it is the body. Why? Because the body will never have the opportunity to regenerate itself if you're constantly feeding it with fear, worry, and dread.

Ironically, I never felt more alive than when I was told I was dying. That's because I am hungry for life. I can choose to dwell on the deadly disease, or I can embrace all that is good, holy, loving, and life-giving.

Choosing life – or any positive emotion – is a choice you must make by intent; it doesn't happen by neglect. In order to choose life, you must become consciously aware of the subconscious thoughts and emotions occupying your mind.

Fear is natural. It's okay to get afraid from time to time; it's just not okay to stay afraid. When fear arises, acknowledge it, and then tell it, "It's time to go. I will not entertain you any longer. Instead, I choose [and name the emotion you wish to embrace]. It may feel silly at first, but you'll soon develop an effective habit of desensitizing fear and anxiety before it debilitates you.

INSIGHT - What are the battles, roadblocks, or challenges you're currently facing in your life and your focus area? Write them down.

Take each one and list how you can feed them with life-giving emotion so you move from obstacles to opportunities?

You feed your own emotions with your own thoughts. Therefore, it requires conscious intent to take every thought captive and make sure it's aligned with all that is positive, constructive, and affirming of your unlimited potential.

Tomorrow we'll look at the number one thing that can sabotage your high-performance goals.

DAY NINETEEN

What "Truths" Are You Telling Yourself?

STORY - I was working with one of the largest trucking companies on driver retention and safety when they had a major AHA moment...

The company's new hires were required to attend driver training institute. As part of their content, instructors reinforced the industry and company averages on accidents – new hires could expect to have some level of accident within the first ninety days.

I shared that we have approximately 50,000 thoughts run across our mind each day. Research suggests most of these thoughts are negative and go unchecked. This internal conversation plus our verbal expressions are known as self-talk. Our self-talk creates pictures in our mind. And we're hard-wired to move toward the most dominant pictures we possess.

Well, if our self-talk creates mental pictures, and we move toward the most dominate pictures we possess, what do think drivers were thinking each time they entered their cab? Is THIS my day?

When instructors realized they were mentally programming drivers toward their own demise, they changed their entire training program and immediately saw accident claims drop significantly in several of their operating centers, well surpassing industry standards.

CONCEPT - "If you keep saying what you have, you'll keep having what you say."

We often talk ourselves right into our own problems. You don't release potential by declaring the problem; you release potential by speaking the solution! Why? You move toward what you think and speak about.

When the company changed their training content, they saw driver accidents decrease 25% in the first three months – a new company and industry record saving them hundreds of thousands of dollars!

INSIGHT - As you think about your focus area today, where is your self-talk potentially killing your progress?

What kinds of mental conversations and verbal communications will move you closer to your goal? Write them down and rehearse them on a daily basis.

Words create pictures in your mind. The pictures you imagine are created from your own self-talk. Interestingly, we don't pay that much attention to the 50,000 thoughts that cross our mind each day. And yet, they determine how your day, your life, and your destiny develop.

Monitoring your self-talk to be positive, constructive, and solution-oriented takes conscious effort. Otherwise, you'll unsuspectingly run into untold accidents putting a costly dent in your future.

DAY TWENTY

A Case of Mistaken Identity

STORY - Tatyana was born in Leningrad in 1989 and abandoned by her birth mother. She lived six years in an orphanage, walking on her hands. Tatyana had spina bifida that paralyzed her from the waist down. Doctors said she was so sick; she'd have little time to live.

American Deborah McFadden adopted Tatyana and brought her to Baltimore. In spite of her circumstances, Tatyana began all types of sports. She started racing competitively at age eight. By 2004 she entered the Summer Paralympics in Athens and won silver and bronze medals. She gained more medals in the 2008 Beijing events. She holds victories in the New York, Chicago, and London marathons. And she's the first athlete to win six gold medals from the IPC Athletics World Championships from 2013.

Tatyana finally returned to her native Russian, this time for the Winter Paralympics at Sochi in 2014. The girl once known for walking on her hands now had arms full of achievement.

CONCEPT - Tatyana wasn't an instant success story. The most formative years of her identity – the first six years of life – were marked with being discarded and dismissed, to say nothing of her physical condition.

Initially, she wasn't allowed to compete in high school sports with able-bodied athletes. She used her embarrassment and rejection as activism for others like her. Her lawsuit against the county created legislation that opened competition to others like her in her state of Maryland.

Though others acted to restrict her self-image, Tatyana didn't let limitations define or deter her. As Eleanor Roosevelt so wisely stated, "No one can make you feel inferior without your consent."

INSIGHT - Take a sheet of paper and draw a line down the middle. At the top of each column write, "I Am."

- Take 60 seconds, and in the first column list all your weaknesses, flaws, or qualities you don't like in yourself – things you'd like to change or improve. Be exhaustive.

- Now, take the next 60 seconds, and in the second column list all your positive strengths, qualities, talents and skills – all those things you like about yourself. Again, list all.

Review both lists. Which list is longer? Which was easier to write?

Examine the negative list. Are there particular voices you hear (parents, siblings, teachers, coaches, managers, spouse, etc.) as you read each one? If so, consider whether their "opinions" became "truths" you accepted and unconsciously adopted.

You build your own self-image with your own thoughts. Your image impacts your level of performance. Then using your self-talk, you critique your performance, reinforcing the image you already hold of yourself.

It's a subconscious self-management cycle that drives and maintains your performance. Tomorrow I'll show you how to stop the cycle so you can build an image that will grow and support your performance at higher levels.

DAY TWENTY-ONE

Managing Your Self Talk

STORY - Yesterday I described the Self-Management Cycle. No matter how people try to label you, you manage your own image with your own thoughts. That image impacts your performance, which you then critique with your self-talk, which reinforces your image, and so it goes.

People with a poor self-image who perform poorly usually sound like this: "Well, there you go. That's just like me. I always mess up." Their own self-talk limits their ability to unleash and utilize more potential.

If their image is bad but they perform well, their self-talk should be positive and uplifting, right? Not necessarily. Typically, it sounds like: "Wow, I can't believe it. That's not like me. I usually goof it up. Must be luck!" With their own negative self-talk, they reject the good and reinforce an already low image.

Conversely, if you hold a high image of yourself but mess up, you'll think: "Wow...I can't believe it. That's not like me. I usually do better. That won't happen again." You reject pervasive failure and reinforce a high image by refusing to accept defeat.

CONCEPT - We possess several different images of ourselves based on the roles we play. For instance, I have one image of myself as a mother, another as a daughter, yet another as a wife, or a friend, an author, neighbor, a consultant, and more.

The image I hold in any one of these areas has everything to do with my estimate and ability to perform well and release higher levels of potential in that role.

Naturally, we all feel better and more confident in our abilities in certain roles over others. The good news is that self-image is something you can develop at higher and higher levels.

According to famed psychologist, Dr. Al Bandura, most people pass through their successes too quickly and too lightly to build a positive, healthy, effective self-image. So one way to build your own self-image and self-efficacy is to reinforce – with your own self-talk – how well you've done. It might sound something like this: "Well, it's just like me to be gentle and patient when the kids start sassing back to me."

When you notice your behaviors, self-talk, or emotions spiraling out of control, don't get down on yourself. Break the cycle. Tell yourself: "STOP! I won't accept this because that's not like me. I can do much better. The next time I expect to ...." Then give yourself the mental picture of the way you want to behave in that situation, the next time. It's a constructive tool to coach yourself (and others) forward.

INSIGHT - Take the 24-hour self-talk challenge. Commit to stopping any negative, sarcastic, belittling language about yourself or others. When it begins to surface, simply say, "Stop! That's not like me. From now on, I'm positive and constructive in all I say and do." Then give yourself the mental picture of the ideal version of you for that particular scenario. Know that failure will come, but don't give up or give in. The more you give your mind the picture of your new behavior; it will eventually become second nature to you.

Self-management is not about ignoring poor or sloppy behavior. But if you continue to dwell on what you did wrong, you're only reinforcing that picture in your mind. Stop the guilt and blame. When things don't go as you'd like, acknowledge that you're better than that. Then give your mind a strong picture of what you intend to do right the next time.

Tomorrow, we'll talk about the importance of mental pictures.

DAY TWENTY-TWO

Discomfort Is Natural

STORY - When teaching, I do a fun, eye-opening exercise with groups. I pass out one card to each participant. On the card is a picture of a lady. I ask those who hold the picture of an old lady to get up and stand on one side of the room. I ask those with the young lady to move to the other side. Then I ask them to cross the room, connect with one person from the other group, and exchange cards. Within minutes, laughter erupts.

You see, they're all holding the same card. But even when they realize it's the same card, they don't necessarily see the other lady in the picture. It can take several minutes to help people identify the opposite lady on their card.

How could they all be looking at the same thing, but see different information?

They're experiencing a principle of cognitive behavior that states: you cannot hold two conflicting thoughts at the same time without tension or anxiety arising. Because your creative subconscious mind doesn't like conflict, it will resolve the problem by causing you to lock onto one idea while blocking out the other.

CONCEPT - Interestingly, the mind doesn't care in which direction it solves the conflict; it simply wants to calm the internal tension. So it moves you toward your most dominant mental picture or belief.

Be careful of the opinions you hold. The more certain you are about your truth, the more difficult it is to see or entertain alternative information. There's no room for growth in the person already full of the answers.

INSIGHT - As you've been thinking about your focus area for these past three weeks, you've likely locked onto ideas or strategies to get you to your goal. Knowing that expertise can be the killer of innovation, where can you open your imagination to new ways of doing things?

Every time you set a new goal, you're creating internal conflict for yourself. What you desire on the outside is a different picture than your current reality on the inside. The tension feels uncomfortable, so your creative subconscious mind engages to fix the problem. How you resolve that discomfort depends on which information is more dominant in your view.

Tomorrow we'll look at how to make the uncomfortable more comfortable so it's easy and natural to navigate toward the new.

DAY TWENTY-THREE

Beyond Comfortable

STORY - We all seek comfort. It's safe, predictable, and familiar. But sometimes we become prisoners of our own comfort, as best depicted in the movie, The Shawshank Redemption, portraying prison life in the 1940's.

Actor Morgan Freeman plays, Red, an inmate serving a life sentence. At one point he describes the subtle transition from freedom to incarceration. He says," At first, these walls, you hate them. They make you crazy. After a while you get used to 'em, don't notice 'em anymore. Then comes the day you realize you need them."

In the movie, Red is finally paroled after serving forty years. Instead of celebrating his freedom he struggles in fear and longs for the familiarity of the walls that had become his home.

CONCEPT - Like a plant, a fish, or a prisoner, you only grow to the size of your container. If you want a bigger life, you'll need a bigger environment. And that often means leaving the level of your comfort zone to move into the capacity of your courage zone.

You can wait for the years of subtle transition or you can jump-start your growth by making the unfamiliar familiar in the imaginations of your mind.

INSIGHT - What new people, places, and experiences might you encounter when you reach your focus area goal? Have fun and expand your imagination. Envision scenarios in your mind now so you can courageously embrace them when they arrive.

Your comfort zones, in every area of your life, represent the range in which you effectively perform. When you move out of your comfort zone, anxiety arises in many forms: accelerated heart rate, cloudy thinking, sweaty palms, stomach acid, and more. All signs warning you to go back to what's "normal" for you.

Continue to spend time visualizing yourself successfully adopting new tasks, attitudes, and opportunities in your goal area that currently cause anxiety arousal. The more familiar they become in your mind, the less discomfort you'll experience when you finally encounter them.

Interestingly it doesn't matter if the behavior or situation is too good for you or not good enough. When you're out of your comfort zone, you get extremely creative and inventive to return to your old way of doing things.

Too many people look forward and scare themselves out of their own future. To expand your comfort zone into your courage zone, you'll need to reframe how you view failure. So tomorrow, I'll show you how.

DAY TWENTY-FOUR

Reframing Failure

STORY - There was a man with huge aspirations. After losing his job, he ran for the state legislature, but was defeated. So he started a business, but that failed. Two years later his fiancée died, and then he had a nervous breakdown. He eventually was elected to his state legislature but was defeated for House Speaker. Five years later he ran for Congress and lost. He finally was elected but lost re-election only two years after that. He was defeated for the US Senate twice in a row, as well as losing the nomination for Vice President. Of his four sons, three died before age eighteen.

In the eyes of most, this man would appear to be a dismal failure. Who in their right mind would aspire to that life?

Thankfully, he did. In 1860, he was elected President of the United States and signed the Emancipation Proclamation, declaring that all slaves would be permanently free. He was, of course, Abraham Lincoln.

CONCEPT - It's said that "Life is 10% what happens to us and 90% what we do with it." Dr Marty Seligman of the University of Pennsylvania and founder of Positive Psychology once said, "It's not our failures that determine our future success, but how we explain them to ourselves.

Henry Ford said it this way, "Failure is the opportunity to begin again more intelligently."

Think on this: success doesn't mean perfect; success simply means seeing it through.

INSIGHT - A wonderful way to build resiliency for yourself, your children, or the people you oversee is to do the following exercise:

Write down 10 big challenges you've experienced in your life that were particularly difficult.

1.

2.

3.

4.

5.

6.

7.

8.

9.

10.

Don't dwell on the pain of the past, but focus on how well you've overcome them. For each, write down specific emotions, strengths, or positive learning lessons you've acquired as a result of being on the other side. Take those emotions of strength, gratitude, courage or more, and cast them forward into your next big endeavor.

Many people look forward and scare themselves right out of their own future. It causes them to lower their goals and expectations. They under-utilize their potential and under-live their life simply because they fear failure.

Fear of failure is actually negative goal setting. It's focusing on what you don't want to happen. Tomorrow I'll show you how to build efficacy and perseverance so you can take on bigger challenges with greater confidence.

DAY TWENTY-FIVE

Don't' Set "Failure" As Your Goal

STORY - Dr. Al Bandura of Stanford University is highly recognized for his decades of research and volumes of work in the area of self-belief or self-efficacy.

Efficacy, defined, is the ability to cause or make happen. Your personal ability to cause or make something happen is known as your "self-efficacy." Subconsciously, there's an immediate, automatic process that takes place every time you encounter new information, opportunities, challenges, or goals. Inside your mind, you go through an instantaneous evaluation of whether or not you're capable of the situation.

If your efficacy is high, you'll naturally gravitate toward it. But if you fear failure or the harsh opinions of others, you'll creatively avoid or dismiss it.

CONCEPT- Growing in efficacy requires you to reframe your idea of failure.

Failure isn't falling down; it's staying down.

It's not getting afraid; it's staying afraid.

Disappointment is inevitable; defeat is not.

Defeat and failure are perspectives you choose.

If you are crippled by other people's criticism, you'll paralyze your own potential.

If you entertain fear and focus on failure, you'll goal-set right into what it is you don't' want.

INSIGHT - Today, dwell on what inspires you about your focus area goal. Write out all the potential benefits – physical, spiritual, financial, relational, emotional and more – that you'll experience as a result. Spend the next week feeling the emotions of achievement and seeing the benefits already accomplished in your mind.

In areas where you find yourself holding back on goals and desires, it's likely you have beliefs, habits, attitudes, expectations, comfort zones or fears you've acquired and assimilated along the way. While you may not be conscious of them, they impact your efficacy, perseverance, and tenacity to move ahead. Identifying what they are and where they are takes thoughtful reflection. Only then can you uproot them and replace them with effective thinking that's aligned with effective goals.

DAY TWENTY-SIX

Going For The Goal

STORY - Research from Virginia Tech offered stunning data on Goal-Setting:

-More than 75% of people don't bother to set goals;

-Of the 25% who do, less than 4% write them down;

-Fewer still – under 1% - review their goals on a regular basis;

-But for that very small percentage who do, they earn up to 9 times more than people who don't set goals at all.

CONCEPT- Here are six critical elements to every effective goal statement:

1. Write it down. Don't worry, you can wordsmith it later.

2. Paint a clear picture. Don't just exercise more. Say what kind and how often. Don't work less hours. Be specific. You want a better life? What does that mean, exactly? If the picture is vague, your motivation will suffer.

3. State what you want, not what you don't want. Too many goals point in the wrong direction and create the wrong picture.

4. Add the benefit factor to your goal using strong vivid words. Why are you bothering to go after this? What's in it for you? Compelling adjectives add emotion necessary to build new memory.

5. Write your goal as already accomplished in the present tense. "I am..." or "I have..." create more of a conflict for your subconscious mind to resolve than "I will" or "I hope to."

6. Read your goals daily. Make them more dominant and desirable than your current reality.

Effective goal-setting takes more than wishful thinking, good intentions, or holiday resolutions. When you write your goals properly and work them daily into your subconscious thinking, you'll find you won't be able to live without the new you.

INSIGHT - Using the six elements for effective goal-setting, write out one or two goals for your focus area.

Transfer each goal statement to a 3 x 5 card or your smart phone. Engage your visual and auditory senses by reading your goals aloud and picturing the end result in your mind at least twice a day.

The difference between those who want a larger life and those who live it is in their ability to create vivid, compelling goals that become more dominant in their thinking than their present reality.

In the next message, I'll show you the most effective way to grow into your new mindset.

DAY TWENTY-SEVEN

Live Your Future Now!

STORY - Throughout the program, I've been helping you identify beliefs, habits, attitudes, expectations, comfort zones, and emotions you currently hold in your subconscious mind that are driving your current outcomes. Your self-talk gives life to and reinforces these belief statements, even if they're blocking your potential for greater success and significance.

Simply trying hard to work or become your new goal statements won't do. That's an external means of pushing behavior that won't last.

The most effective way to create new behaviors is to create new truths for yourself, or statements of fact known as Affirmations.

Affirmations are new beliefs, written in the same goal format, that you'll need in order to support and accomplish your goal.

Affirmations declare end-result thinking. It's not "I can" or "I will," but "I am!" It's a done deal...now!

"The game is won" - before I've already played it. "I am healed" - before there's any medical evidence to prove it. "We have the account" – before you've picked up the phone to make the appointment. That's how you speak to yourself.

CONCEPT - We live in a world that claims, "Seeing is believing." But in fact, the opposite is true – You believe and then you see. You don't see first. The more you understand how the mind works, the bolder your goal setting becomes and the greater your potential to live the life you desire.

INSIGHT - Take your goal statements. Now write 3-5 affirmations (or new truths) you'll need to believe in order to support your goal. Typically you want several new beliefs to support the emotional, financial, relational, physical, education, etc., aspects of your goal. Like your goals, speak them aloud at least twice each day.

If you can affirm it, you can achieve it. The key is training yourself in end-result thinking. Most people put their goals and affirmations in the future tense. They want to, hope to, wish to, will. I see these words time and again as I coach people in goal-setting. Future tense goals rarely work.

The idea is to intentionally create a conflict in your system so your creative subconscious will fix the problem. Tomorrow I'll share how to make sure you fix the problem in the direction you desire.

DAY TWENTY-EIGHT

Your Mind Doesn't Know the Difference

STORY - Goal-Setting is intentionally creating conflict for yourself. Your goal, made consciously, is for outcomes different than what you know to be true about yourself subconsciously. Because sanity of mind is more important than success, your creative subconscious senses the conflict and jump-starts to fix the problem. It gives you just enough drive, energy, motivation, and ideas to do so. In fact, you're at your creative best when you set a new goal or have a problem.

Because the mind is amoral (it simply records what you give it), it doesn't care in which direction it solves the problem. It simply drives toward the most dominant picture you hold in your mind – what's "normal" for you.

So how do you make your goals and end-result affirmations more "normal" than your current reality? Through the practice of visualization....building new pictures that create "new normals" in your mind.

CONCEPT - Your mind doesn't know the difference between what's real and what you tell it. Therefore, as you live your goals and affirmations in your mind, first, you'll naturally gravitate toward the outcomes you desire.

Research indicates that reading your goals and affirmations on a regular basis makes a 25% impact on your subconscious beliefs. Reading and picturing your goals regularly makes a

55% impact in building new beliefs. But reading, picturing, and feeling your end-result makes a 100% impact toward creating new memory with emotion.

Doing this twice a day over a 30-day period will begin to build new beliefs that shift your thinking and create new behaviors.

INSIGHT - Today – start your morning and end your day by reading, visualizing, and feeling the end-result of your goal and affirmation statements. Take just one minute on each. Be relaxed, close your eyes, and enjoy the feelings associated with each achievement.

Each time you read, picture, and feel your affirmations, it's like creating a 1-minute commercial in your mind. The more you visualize your new beliefs, the more familiar and comfortable they'll become over your old, ineffective ones.

All high-performing people think this way....they see their end-result desires more clearly and more dominantly than their current circumstances. But not all outcomes are healthy, constructive, or equitable. Tomorrow we'll examine why.

DAY TWENTY-NINE

BE UNIQUELY OUTSTANDING!

STORY - Science-fiction writer, Ray Bradbury, wrote:

"Everyone must leave something behind when he dies, my grandfather said. A child or a book or a painting or a house or a wall built or a pair of shoes made. Or a garden planted. Something your hand touched some way so your soul has somewhere to go when you die, and when people look at that tree or that flower you planted, you're there.

It doesn't matter what you do, he said, so long as you change something from the way it was before you touched it into something that's like you after you take your hands away. The difference between the man who just cuts lawns and a real gardener is in the touching, he said. The lawn-cutter might just as well not have been there at all; the gardener will be there a lifetime."

CONCEPT - It's not what you do, but how you do it that determines the quality of your touch.

Living from a place of contributory purpose rather than a random array of whims, desires, obligations, or accomplishments is one of the most common attributes of uniquely outstanding individuals.

They live with an absolute sense of mission in mind.

Their picture of purpose becomes the foundation for their life and filter for their goals.

Their motivation isn't from what they gain, but in what they give to the world around them.

INSIGHT - Think about the legacy you'd like to leave. What is it you hope people will say of you?

When others look back on your life, what qualities, characteristics and values will they talk about? Write them down and begin visualizing these attributes into your goals.

Don't wait for the end of your life to think about how you wish you had lived your life. Success author Stephen Covey wrote, "Begin with the end in mind." Based on his "7 Habits of Highly Effective People," take a minute and write your own eulogy or obituary as you hope it would be written about you. Then take a moment each day or week to read it. You'll begin to experience a transformation of mind and spirit that brings fullness into all you do.

Simply having the power to harness your mind for more falls far short of your potential. History is full of mission-minded people whose legacy is marred with selfishness, hate, and destruction.

We've been endowed with accountability and responsibility to steward the resources of this world and create a common good for all. To that end, your potential is your deposit for continuous improvement as an uniquely outstanding individual.

DAY THIRTY

Reaching New Heights

STORY - A pilot climbed into his single-manned plane and flew off, leaving the earth far behind as he soared above the clouds.

After reaching cruising altitude, he removed his helmet and noticed a strange noise, like a gnawing on rubber or plastic. To his horror, below the instrument panel was a rat, out of his reach and chewing on the electrical cord between the plane's controls and engine. If the rat were to cut through the line, the plane would careen out of control and crash immediately.

His first instinct was to descend – get his wheels on the ground with an emergency landing. But he had flown too high and there wouldn't be enough time to reach the earth. So in a split-second decision, he chose to ascend....go even higher. The pilot put on his oxygen mask, boosted power to the plane's engine, and quickly climbed as high as he and the plane could go.

Soon the gnawing sound ended, and the pilot began his decent. When he landed, he found the rat....DEAD.

CONCEPT - You are fearfully and wonderfully made with unlimited potential for continuous horizons of improvement. You now have tools and insights to soar even higher into your next-level living.

Along the way, problems will surely threaten to disrupt or derail you. People afraid of heights will try to drag you down to an altitude more comfortable for them.

Don't back down your dreams or destiny. Look up and go higher. Your challenges won't survive the climb.

INSIGHT - Congratulations! You've just spent the last 30 days moving toward the goal in a focus area of your life. If you want to sustain energy and motivation, begin now to create a new target goal. You're ready for the stretch. What's that next-level horizon for you? Dream big and write it down.

Once you've reached your goal, your creative subconscious shuts off drive, energy, and motivation. Why? There's no more problem. No goal....no conflict. No conflict....no energy needed.

So start a new problem. You're an endless reservoir of potential just waiting to find solutions.

Albert Einstein said, "No problem can be solved on the same level of consciousness that created it." By harnessing the power of your mind, there are no limits to the levels you can reach!

WELL DONE

Congratulations on completing your 30 day journey from potential to performance!

Mentioned earlier in the content, Dr. Al Bandura stated that most of us pass through our successes too quickly and too lightly in order for them to build our self-image and grow our efficacy. Using the formula of Recall x Repetition = Belief (or new memory), take this important step of recalling impactful learning lessons that brought light to ineffective thinking. Before you bring this process to a close, write down the major concepts that impacted you:

Now describe the personal insights you gained from each concept:

As a result of your new knowledge and revelations, make a list of those things you plan to do differently:

In order to maintain drive, creativity, and energy, there must be a goal. What new goals or changes would you like to achieve next? Where do you go from here?

Though you've reached the end of the 30 learning lessons, this journal is an active resource you can return to time and again. Each time you want to take on a new area of growth and development, you can use this 30-day process to discover root cause attitudes, habits, beliefs, and expectations producing your current results, and then apply the cognitive and physiological principles for creating more effective thinking patterns that will move you to the next level.

Learning and assimilation come through repetition. The daily messages will remind you of important life and leadership principles. The reflection activities are living questions that will ignite new insights as your internal and external environments change around you.

One of the best ways to learn and retain information is to teach it. Consider using these questions as meeting starters with your family, colleagues, or community groups so you can engage others, grow collaboration, win trust, and build group efficacy. Then watch your success and significance continue to expand!

Doreen Lecheler

Maximizing Personal Growth, Influential Leadership Behaviors, and Cultures of Continuous Improvement

Doreen is a capacity-builder, goal-setting expert, international speaker, and best-selling author. Best of all, she's an "incurable" cancer conqueror who gets to live her passion and purpose - growing people and transforming cultures. Whether working with leaders of a nation, community, organization or team, Doreen's work turns meaningful potential into measurable performance by unfolding the process for how to manage your mind.

Doreen began her career in the mid-1980s, helping to progress several start-up nonprofits into regionally, nationally, and internationally recognized organizations. She held senior leadership positions overseeing growth in program development, business development, and organizational advancement.

Since 2000, Doreen has consulted in business, government, education, nonprofits, and athletics, using researched-based tools and techniques for transformation and sustainable goal achievement. Doreen has facilitated high-performance results in the areas of building cultures of excellence, leadership, and team development, change management, employee engagement, goal setting, and vision building. She is a certified speaker for the CEO group, Vistage International.

Doreen has authored two books on personal and professional development. *Growing from Potential to Performance* and *The*

Influence Zone: Leadership Intelligence that Ignites Results each provide 30-days of inspiration, learning lessons, and reflection activities designed to upgrade the level of thinking, behavior, and meaningful, measurable results.

Doreen's ability to guide outstanding personal achievement never became more critical than in 2009 with a cancer recurrence staged as "incurable" with metastases to the bone. Aligning life-producing principles of body, mind, and spirit, Doreen experienced miraculous healing with no metastatic evidence of cancer. She fervently shares her cancer-conquering strategies to help others overcome challenges and roadblocks that inhibit well-being and success. She is the author of two books on faith and healing. Her last work, *The Mind to Heal*, was an immediate Amazon inspirational bestseller. She is also the creator of the spiritual growth program, *Destiny Living: Receiving God's Heart for Your Purpose-Filled Potential*.

Doreen has been a Senior Consultant with The Pacific Institute and Excellent Cultures. She holds a degree in Business from the University of Maryland and a master's degree in Theology/Counseling from Wesley Theological Seminary.

www.DoreenLecheler.com

The Influence Zone
Leadership Intelligence That Ignites Results

Do you consciously consider how your interactions affect those around you or whether your behavior will help facilitate the best possible outcomes imaginable? Most people don't. They simply react or respond in the moment with subconscious impulses and attitudes.

If you're not choosing your words, actions, and attitudes with thoughtful intent then you're likely acting from spontaneous habit or mindless neglect. The choices you make determine the maximum radius of your impact, otherwise known as your "Influence Zone."

Head-smarts alone will only take you so far. To achieve inspirational impact, cooperation, and optimum effect, you must connect in ways that engage others toward mutually rewarding, purpose-driven outcomes. Whether you're a parent, teacher, coach or organizational leader, *The Influence Zone* will guide you through 30 days of personal insight into roadblocks inhibiting your impact, as well as the neurocognitive tools to grow your success.

www.DoreenLecheler.com

More titles by Doreen Lecheler

For over 30 years Doreen has helped individuals and organizations turn potential into performance, not realizing that one day she'd be using these methods in the fight for her life. She is a stage four, breast cancer conqueror.

The Spirit to Heal

When Doreen was diagnosed with a breast cancer recurrence in 2009, she wasn't prepared to hear that it was now "incurable," stage four, with metastases to the bone. One prominent institution gave her one year before the metastases would be throughout her body.

As a peak-performance consultant and goal-setting expert, Doreen knew she needed a target. As a faithful Christian, she didn't know which target was meant for her. In her first book, Doreen discovers the truth of what to think in the midst of disease. It is her journey of discovery and faith in the God who seeks to save.

The Mind to Heal

Amazon #1 Inspirational Hot New Releases
Amazon #2 Inspirational Best-Seller

Doreen combines the power of faith with the neurocognitive science of goal-setting and effective thinking skills in this powerful book. Using her own cancer experience, Doreen prescribes seven critical choices necessary to create an environment for healing, health, and wellness. THE MIND to HEAL focuses on how to think in the midst of disease.

Receiving God's Heart For Your Purpose-Filled Potential

In **DESTINY LIVING**, Doreen brings research from performance psychology, along with biblical principles from God's heart to us, to overcome obstacles and create steps for purpose-filled living. She combines the psychology of break-through thinking with the transformational power of identity and inheritance to create change that is both successful and significant.

For individuals or small groups, **DESTINY LIVING** is a twelve-unit, self-paced program with reflection activities at the end of each unit. The program promotes self-discovery and group dialogue to create engagement with the information and reinforcement of the learning concepts.

12-unit audio program or DVD series, including
Destiny Living workbook

www.DestinyMakers.org
Office@DestinyMakers.org